This Walker book belongs to

_____

_____

_____

I am Paulo Marcelo Feliciano,
and soon I will shine like a star.
I will light up the homes in this favela.
I will light every home in Brazil.

Like Garrincha, Pelé and Ronaldo,
who have all played in these alleys,
I will play my way to stardom,
because I'm a champion, too.

# Football Star

## Mina Javaherbin    illustrated by Renato Alarcão

### AUTHOR'S NOTE

In Brazil, some children work hard for a living to overcome a stubborn opponent: poverty. This experience of life's hardship, of being engaged in the survival arena from childhood, has helped shape Brazil's solid team of stars shining at the top of the world of football. My story is a homage to all football stars who have risen and continue to rise up from poverty.

*To Mom and Dad*
*M. J.*

*To the Brazilian kids who once dreamed of becoming football stars*
*R. A.*

**WALKER BOOKS**
AND SUBSIDIARIES
LONDON · BOSTON · SYDNEY · AUCKLAND

First published 2014 by Walker Books Ltd. 87 Vauxhall Walk, London SE11 5HJ · 2 4 6 8 10 9 7 5 3 1 · Text © 2014 Mina Javaherbin · Illustrations © 2014 Renato Alarcão · The right of Mina Javaherbin and Renato Alarcão to be identified as author and illustrator respectively of this work has been asserted by them in accordance with the Copyright, Designs and Patents Act 1988 · This book has been typeset in ITC Fenice · Printed in China · All rights reserved. No part of this book may be reproduced, transmitted or stored in an information retrieval system in any form or by any means, graphic, electronic or mechanical, including photocopying, taping and recording, without prior written permission from the publisher. · British Library Cataloguing in Publication Data: a catalogue record for this book is available from the British Library · ISBN 978-1-4063-5382-2 (hbk) 978-1-4063-5721-9 (pbk) · www.walker.co.uk

I am Paulo Marcelo Feliciano
and when I'm a football star,
my mother won't have to work long hours
and I won't have to miss her so much.

All day, I help Senhor da Silva fish.
After work, I practise soccer with him.

At night my sister, Maria, and I
read and write and play.
I teach her football moves;

she teaches me maths from school.

This morning, Mamãe left me enough *pão de queijo*
to share with my football team.
We'll need the energy tonight.
We have a big game on the beach!

I swallow my cheese buns and pack some for Maria.
We run out of the door to her school.

And we dribble past our neighbourhood.

I kick the ball to Maria.
She heads it back to me.

I pass the ball to Maria again,
and this time she knees it up.

I kick it past her little shoulders.
She fires her bicycle kick!

Maria sees that I'm impressed.
"So *now* can I be on your team?"

She asks me this day after day.
But my answer is always the same:
"Our team's rule is *no girls.*"

Maria looks sad, so I say,
"We'll practise more after my game, OK?"
She smiles a little, waves goodbye
and walks to her class.

I dribble to Carlos, who's shining shoes
with his sisters by his side.
I know that one day, his fancy footwork
will score us brilliant goals.

I leave a bun for my goalie, Jose.
He is diving for tourists this morning.
I know that one day, he will dive for the ball
and take our team to the top.

I dribble to Givo, who helps the dancers
and works on the carnival floats.
I know that one day, he will dance with the ball
and the fans will cheer his moves.

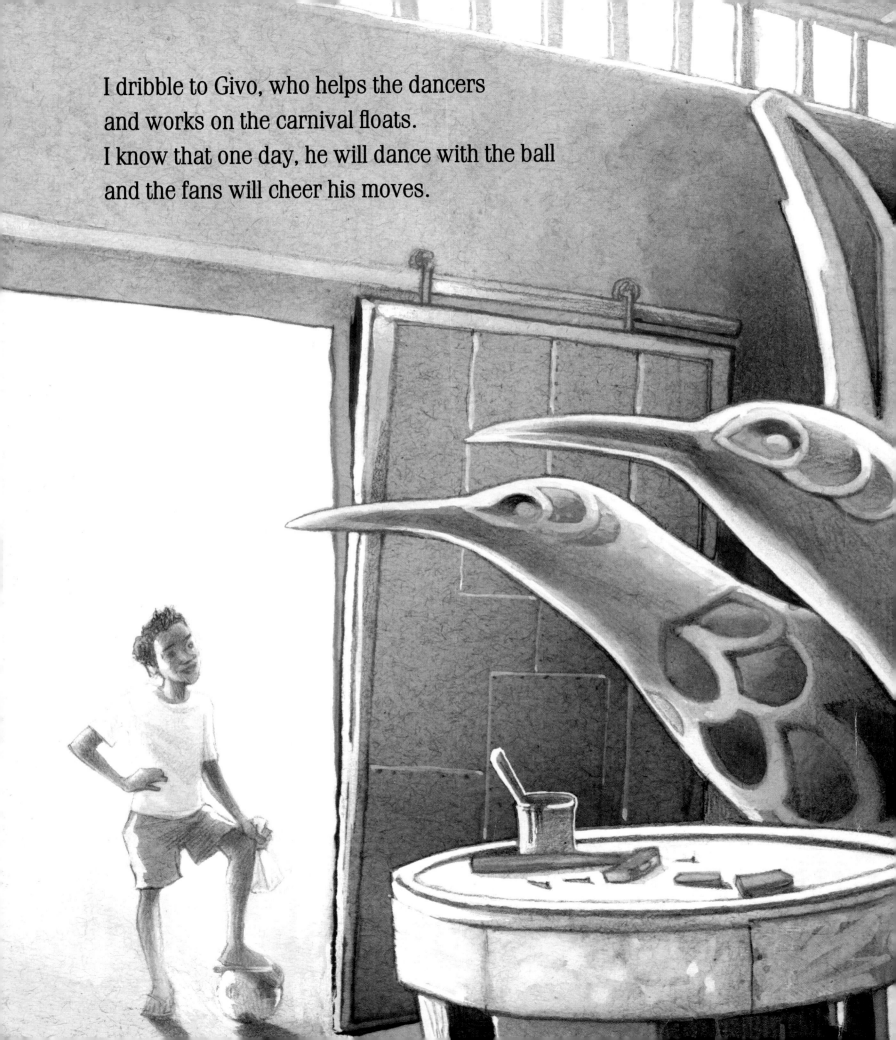

I dribble to Pedro, at the coconut grove.
He is climbing up a tree.
I know that one day, he'll climb to glory
and harvest us fortune and trophies.

I am Paulo Marcelo Feliciano.
I will lead my team to the top
and the crowd will cheer my football name:

"Captain Felino! The star!"

"Felino! Hurry! You're late!" Senhor da Silva shouts.

We're off to the ocean, and when it's time,
I cast my net in the deep.
Wild storm clouds
appear fast
in the sky above.

Over and over, I cast the net.
I gather and pull in the catch.
Senhor da Silva and I discuss
my game plans for tonight.
I keep an eye on the horizon
and hope that the clouds will disappear.

Senhor da Silva finally says, "Felino,
enough for today."
The grey clouds suddenly sail away —
away from the beach,
away from my game.

We steer the boat to the shore,
and my team gathers to help.

We plan and practise our game.

Jose will fly,

Givo will bounce,

Carlos will kick,

Pedro will shoot ...

and Felino will score!

Maria arrives, along with two of Carlos's sisters,
and the other team arrives too.

My sister runs to my teammates and asks,
"Please can I play on your team?"
"She's really good!" I say with a grin,
and Carlos's sisters cheer.
But the boys cross their arms, say no, and frown.
"Not this time," I say to Maria.

The game starts.
Their forward attacks.

Jose jumps up and – *whoosh!*

He lands on his wrist.
I run over to him.
"The wrist isn't broken," Senhor da Silva says,
"but I think Jose should rest."

Givo stands in as goalie,
and we're a player short.

"Maria?" I ask my team.
Givo votes no,
Pedro votes yes
and Carlos is fine either way.

It's up to me,
and my vote is for change.
I wave to my sister and say, "It's time!"
and Maria runs onto the field.

Maria runs all over the field.
She heads to Pedro,
she knees to Carlos ...
and when the ball flies
past her little shoulders,
she fires her bicycle kick

## and she scores!

I am Paulo Marcelo Feliciano,
the captain of this team.
No storm, fall, or useless old rule
can keep us from a win.

Our fans will one day call us the stars.
We will light up every home in Brazil.

**Mina Javaherbin** was born in Iran and now lives in the USA, in California, where she works as an architect. She likes to look for what we share, and sometimes calls herself a world citizen. She is also the author of *Goal!*, illustrated by A. G. Ford. "Football is magic to me," Mina says. "Where there is a ball, there's hope, laughter and strength."

**Renato Alarcão** has illustrated many children's books. He lives in Brazil.

## Also by Mina Javaherbin:

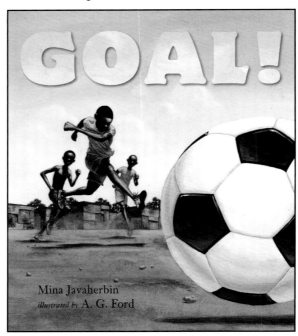

978-1-4063-2771-7

Available from all good booksellers

www.walker.co.uk